E

Library of Congress Cataloging in Publication Data
Yabuuchi, Masayuki, 1940-
Whose footprints?

Translation of: Nani no ashiato ka na.
Summary: Depicts the footprints of a duck, cat, bear, horse, hippopotamus, and goat.
1. Animal tracks—Juvenile literature. |1. Animal tracks| I. Title.
QL768.Y3313   1985   599   84-1087
ISBN 0-399-21209-4

Published in the United States in 1985 by Philomel Books.
A division of The Putnam Publishing Group,
51 Madison Avenue, New York, NY 10010.
Printed in Japan.
Originally published in Japan in 1983 by
Fukuinkan Shoten Publishers, Inc., Tokyo.

Whose Footprints?

Masayuki Yabuuchi

PHILOMEL BOOKS
New York

Two webbed footprints.
Whose are they?

They belong to a duck.

Four toes and a pad —
whose footprints are these?

They belong to a cat.

This is a hoofprint.
Whose could it be?

It belongs to a goat.

17

Here's another hoofprint.
Can you guess whose it is?

It belongs to a horse.

Five sharp claws on this footprint.
Whose is it?

It's a bear's footprint.

This footprint must belong to
a large, heavy animal.
Is it an elephant?

No! It's a hippopotamus!